INSANE SPEED

STREET BIKE MANIA

Craig Stevens

A Crabtree Seedlings Book

CRABTREE
Publishing Company
www.crabtreebooks.com

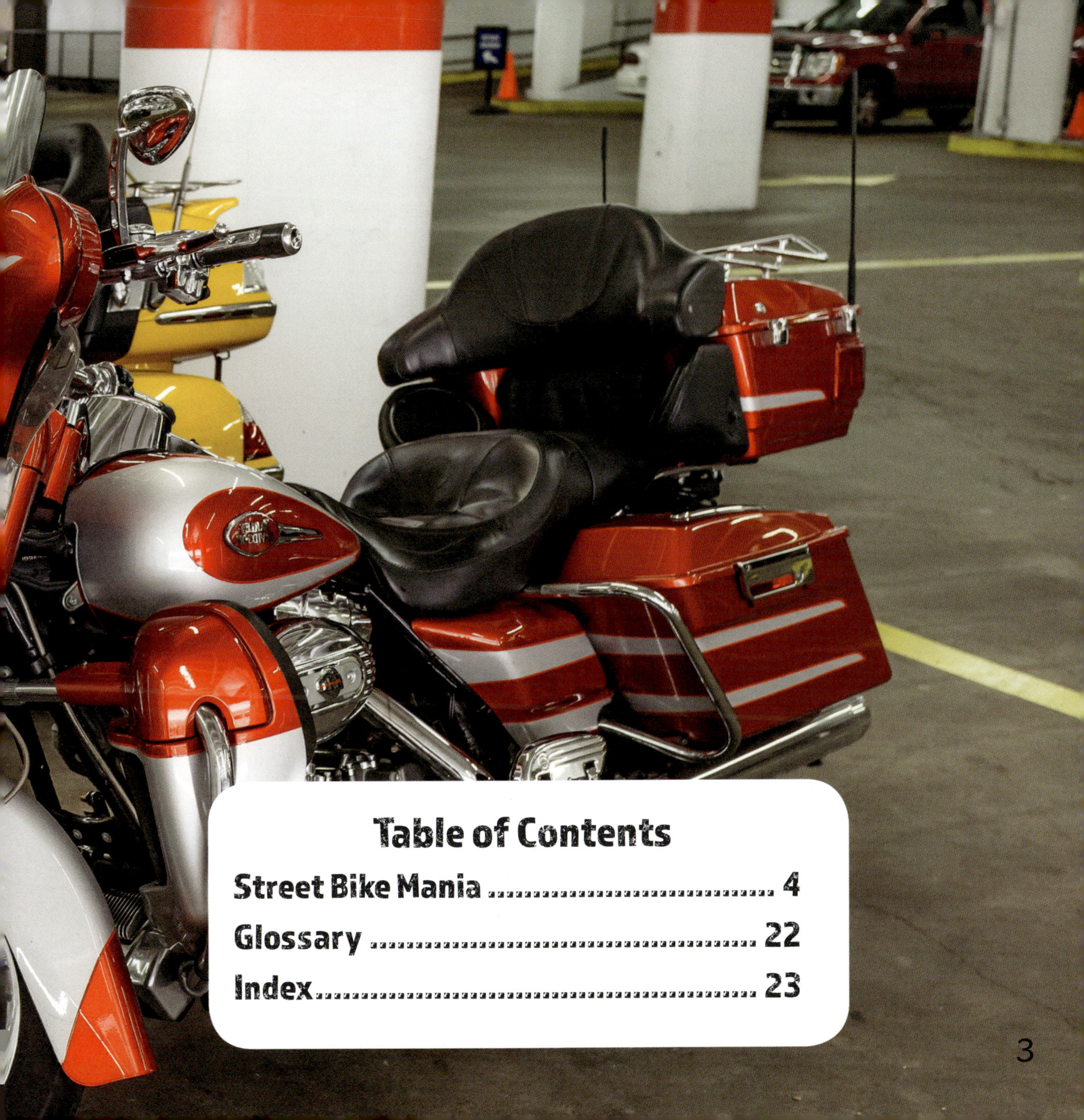

Table of Contents

Street Bike Mania

Street bikes are a great way to get around.

They are easy to park and use less gas than a car.

Most people ride them because they are fast and fun.

Sport bikes are made for speed and sharp turns.

gas tank - holds over 4.4 gallons (17 liters) of gas
seat - room for rider and passenger
rear brake light - warns drivers behind you when to slow or stop
muffler - reduces noise of exhaust being released
CB1100

handlebars - for steering; also holds rearview mirror and controls for the throttle (power) and clutch to change gears
headlight and turn signals - for safe driving
front shocks - help make the ride smoother when going over bumps
street tires - good tread to grip the road
front brakes - stop the bike
engine - large and powerful

A **clutch** lever and gears **engage** the chain to turn the rear wheel. This makes the bike go.

Some street bikes have **storage compartments**.

storage compartment

12V
km/h

Street bikes have **gauges** that show how fast the bike is moving and how much gas is left.

They also have brake lights, headlights, and turn signals.

429B49

approved helmet
eye protection
leather jacket
long pants
solid shoes or boots

The right clothing is important to ride safely.

Glossary

clutch (KLUCH): A clutch is a lever in a car or on a motorcycle that you press to change gears.

engage (en-GAYJ): To engage something is to set it into operation.

gauges (GAYJ-ez): Gauges are devices that are made for measuring. A gas gauge measures how much gas is in a car or motorcycle tank.

sport bikes (SPORT BIKES): Sport bikes are street bikes that are made for fast speeds and handling corners and turns on the road.

storage compartments (STOR-ij kuhm-PART-muhnts): Storage compartments are containers that you can keep things in.

street bikes (STREET BIKES): Street bikes are any motorcycles that people are allowed to ride on public roads.

Index

School-to-Home Support for Caregivers and Teachers

This book helps children grow by letting them practice reading. Here are a few guiding questions to help the reader build his or her comprehension skills. Possible answers appear here in red.

Before Reading

- **What do I think this book is about?** I think this book is about riding a street bike. I think this book is about the correct clothing to wear on a street bike.
- **What do I want to learn about this topic?** I want to learn more about how fast a street bike can go. I want to learn if there is a difference between a street bike and a motorcycle.

During Reading

- **I wonder why...** I wonder why someone would rather have a street bike than a car. I wonder why many street bike riders wear black leather jackets.
- **What have I learned so far?** I have learned that street bikes have brake lights, headlights, and turn signals. I have learned that a clutch is a lever on a street bike that you press to change gears.

After Reading

- **What details did I learn about this topic?** I have learned that street bikes have gas gauges that measures how much gas is in the tank. I have learned that you should wear an approved helmet when you ride on a street bike.
- **Read the book again and look for the glossary words.** I see the word *engage* on page 12, and the word *gauges* on page 17. The other glossary words are found on pages 22 and 23.

Library and Archives Canada Cataloguing in Publication

CIP available at Library and Archives Canada

Library of Congress Cataloging-in-Publication Data

CIP available at Library of Congress

Crabtree Publishing Company
www.crabtreebooks.com 1–800–387–7650

Written by: Craig Stevens

Print coordinator: Katherine Berti

Printed in the U.S.A./CG20210915/012022

Print book version produced jointly with Blue Door Education in 2022

PHOTO CREDITS:
www.shutterstock.com, www.istockphoto.com, COVER: Jag_cz-shutterstock.com; Title page, Pages 9, 22: Michal Vitek-shutterstock.com; Pages 2-3: typhoonski-istockphoto.com; Page 4: AlexLinch-istockphoto.com; Page 5: mihaperosa-istockphoto.com; Page 6: DianeBentleyRaymond-istockphoto.com; Pages 7, 23: DTatiana8-istockphoto.com; Pages 8, 10-11: honda.com; Pages 12, 22: Baldube-shutterstock.com; Pages 13, 22: oneinchpunch-istockphoto.com; Pages 14, 23: Aljndr-istockphoto.com; Page 15: egon69-istockphoto.com; Pages 16-17, 22: djedzura -istockphoto.com; Page 18: Lukas Gojda-shutterstock.com; Page 19: vtwinpixel-istockphoto.com; Pages 20-21: JohanJK-istockphoto.com

Published in the United States
Crabtree Publishing
347 Fifth Ave.
Suite 1402-145
New York, NY 10016

Published in Canada
Crabtree Publishing
616 Welland Ave.
St. Catharines, Ontario
L2M 5V6